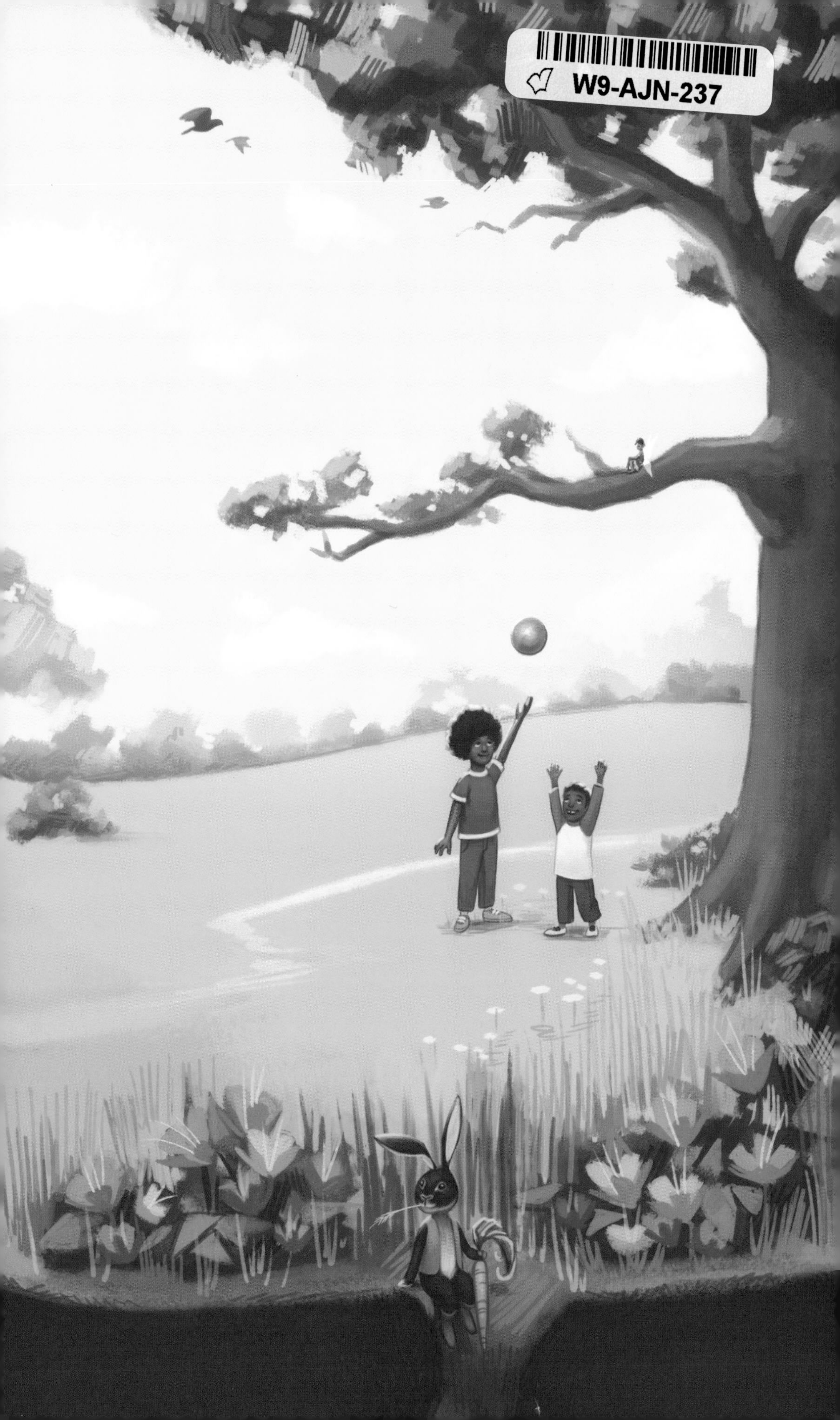

FOR ALL THE BELIEVERS

FIRST EDITION
10 9 8 7 6 5 4 3 2 1

PUBLISHED BY BSF BOOKS AND STRANGER COMICS, LLC
PRINTED IN SOUTH KOREA

WWW.BROWNSUGARFAIRIES.COM

BROWN SUGAR
FAIRIES

WRITTEN AND CREATED BY
AIYSHA SINCLAIR

DRAWN BY
JOYCELINE FURNISS

EDITED BY
JOSHUA COZINE

"YOU, MY DARLING, ARE MAGIC."

~EFG

The Tallest True Tales

At ten years old, Peppa was the oldest of three siblings and the only child on her block who didn't run to the pool every day to escape the summer heat. She had an inquisitive mind and a smart mouth that often made keeping friends hard to do. Instead, she'd retreat from her younger brothers to her own room, a sanctuary of books that looked more like a library than a bedroom. Although odd in shape, they stacked neatly in the bookcase her papa had made her. Within these four walls, underneath a makeshift tent she'd made up top her bed, she would escape into worlds made of magic and adventure, one page at a time.

Just about every gift-giving holiday, Peppa's parents would donate a brand new book to her collection. She had "Alice's Adventures," "The Sea of Adventure," "The Island of Adventure," and a few folk-tales Grandma had brought her from back home in Louisiana.

Not long ago, you see, Peppa's grandfather had taken

ill, and it was too much for her grandmother, so both of them moved in with Peppa's family. "It's only until he is well enough to go back home," Grandma would say, but Grandpa never agreed. He never said or did much of anything, in fact. Seemed the only thing that could make him light up was when Peppa practiced his favorite Jazz tune, "Lady Bird," on her flute. Peppa loved her grandpa more than anything, so she played his song anytime he wanted to hear it. The way his eyes turned young again made it just fine by her.

Days seemed to move as slow as dripping molasses for Peppa that summer. She often entertained herself by getting into trouble on purpose, usually for being late to the dinner table. "I'm sorry, Mama, but Alice fell into the well again chasing after that white rabbit. Don't you think it rather rude of me to just leave her there?" she would protest, but all coy and sweet. Peppa thought it funny to blame it on the characters from her stories. Well… her mama didn't think it was worth a chuckle and got good and fed up with Peppa's tales and trying tongue.

"Peppa, honey, I spoke with Mrs. Bowers today and she was going on about how she could use some extra help around the market. Wouldn't be a bad idea for you to go on down there a couple days a week and lend a hand," suggested Mama in a way that wasn't a suggestion at all. "I've already made the arrangements for you to start tomorrow morning, and no foolishness. Or there'll be no new books to read."

Mrs. Bowers was an old family friend who owned a market in the village square. She had a reputation for having the best sweet bread in town, but that wasn't the only reason folks came to see her. She was known to be

able to interpret the most scrambled up dreams, and she'd do it if you gave her a trinket for her store. On Sundays after church, you'd find a line as long as a hundred snakes tied together holding all kinds of treasures from cooking pots to ancient masks, and books, of course! Come rain or shine, the whole town would be waiting for a slice of sweet bread heaven, a dream reading, and a pep talk to get them through the week.

"You hear me, girl?"

"Yes, Mama," Peppa said as only children can.

Little did she know, Peppa was being sent out to solve one of the greatest mysteries of her life. Well… up until that day at least.

The Detective's First Day

When morning arrived, Peppa reluctantly made her way to the shirt and pants her mama had neatly pressed and laid out the night before. All dressed and on her way down the dusty Old Dale Road on an already hot and sunny day, Peppa skipped and jumped over the last puddles left by the late night rain. When she got to the big front door of the market, Peppa noticed a basket toppled over on its side. With a curious eye, she peaked inside to find two bananas, a spilt jar of grape jelly, and a roll of that delicious sweet bread.

Peppa glanced around to see if the person who left it behind was possibly standing nearby, but no one was in sight. So she picked up the basket and entered the market store where she found Mrs. Bowers already dusting. The shop was a well-organized jumble of what everyday folks need to get through life: food, tools, some clothes, and a great big jar of licorice sticks. Behind the menagerie, there stood three doors. One led behind the shop, another to the

kitchen, and the last was a big brown door with a big old sign that read PRIVATE. It was the reading room.

Mrs. Bowers was a rather round woman who stood no taller than the 4 foot deli counter. She wore one thick boot on her small left foot to help with balance. Wooden step stools were placed every few feet behind the counter. As small as she was, this tiny woman had a voice so loud she filled every room of the mart without the need of a speaker.

"Good morning, Peppa," she greeted with a smile as big as her laugh. "So glad you made it here safely. I was sure that last night's rain was going to wash us all away. But look, the wind pushed it aside and made way for sunshine! Ooooh and the smell of sweet lilac in the air! Do you like lilac?" she asked, but continued on dusting without giving breath to an answer from Peppa. It was just like being at home, Peppa thought.

Mrs. Bowers gave Peppa her duties for the day. She was to make a list of items that were on the bottom shelves, restock them, make note of expired food, and write a list of what needed to be reordered.

Still holding the basket of fruit and bread, "Um, Mrs. Bowers..." mumbled Peppa. "I found this outside the shop. Looks like someone left it there over night cause it's kinda wet. What should I do with it?"

With much caution, Mrs, Bowers carefully peered inside the basket, worried it was a mouse or something. "Hmmnn!" she huffed. "Well, it's of no good use to me! The bread's all soggy and someone already nibbled on the bananas, plus it's leaking water all over my floor! Go on and take it out back to the trash and throw that stuff away."

"You got it!" replied Peppa. So just as she was instructed, Peppa made her way to the trash bins outside in the back alleyway. But with each step, her investigative nature started to bubble inside. She couldn't help but wonder who could have left the basket behind with all those treats. It was all rather suspicious, made all the more so by the fact that it was an otherwise dull day, so of course Peppa was determined to find the culprit.

"Maybe there's a clue inside the basket?" she quizzed out loud. Examining each item, one by one, she tossed them into the trash until... she stopped at the last banana. Not only had it been nibbled on, but it was also covered in some sort of sticky purple goop. With her pinky finger, she scooped the goop and stuck it in her mouth to see if it was grape jelly.

"Yuck!" she blurted. "That doesn't taste like any jelly I've ever had! This is surely a clue. I'm gonna have to follow the goop!"

Looking around, Peppa noticed little purple splashes leading back inside the store. Her eyes followed splotches along the shelf wall and up to the top of the doorway that led inside Mrs. Bowers' reading room. Now, Peppa knew good and well that opening a closed door with the huge sign that read PRIVATE was not a good idea. But she couldn't help herself, and was compelled, like a detective in one of her favorite adventure stories, to go inside and have a snoop around.

Sneaking quickly inside, the door creaked in turmoil behind her. Peppa held her breath for a shout from Mrs. Bowers… that never came. She let out a sigh of relief and

took in the wonders of the room thanks to a soft warm glow from the outside sun. It was filled with lots of dusty old books, and colorful fabrics draped on the windows, where wind chimes hung waiting for a breeze. But in the center, next to an old armchair, was the room's most precious jewel; a golden crystal ball was gloriously displayed on a small round table.

"Wow," she gasped, "Mrs. Bowers must know a lot about magical things." But Peppa, of course, was more interested in the books. There were all types, from little diaries to novels to big old tomes, some with funny names that Peppa couldn't quite pronounce.

"Must be Creole," she figured, thumbing the spines to get a better read. "Grandma Nelly has a few like this in her house in Louisiana."

Full of excitement, she moved like the wind from one to the next, but the dust from the books made Peppa sneeze three times. She stepped back and bumped a shelf, knocking a thick red book off its old wooden surface. It fell with a THUD, but this time Peppa didn't wait for Mrs. Bowers to scream. She was too excited. She had found a clue!

"Gotcha!" she beamed, observing the sticky purple goop on the edge of the big book. On the dark red cover were pretty letters in gold that spelled S A R O J A. Below them was a beautiful golden flower unlike any Peppa had ever seen. But the book was sticky to the touch. It gave Peppa a fight when she tried to open it, a fight that she lost. Had the goop fused the pages together, she wondered, or did the book have a mind of its own? Nervous now, but even more curious, she gave it another try, pulling with all of her might.

Nothing!

She hopped on the table, knees to chest, with both hands on the cover, forcing the book wide open… with an explosion of sparkling dust splashing on her face.

Clumsily gathering herself, she took off her glittery glasses, and then something caught the corner of her eye. Squinting tightly, she thought she saw a flutter of iridescent wings escaping to hide behind the crystal ball. Her mouth fell wide with amazement as she moved in closer, peering through the ball. Those two wings were attached to two arms and two legs! Two little hands moved, revealing the face of the tiniest little being she had ever seen. A pair of frightened eyes stared back at her.

Yup, right there in front of her was a teeny, tiny, exceptionally beautiful fairy girl. Her skin was glowing cinnamon with stripes of paint, and miniature wild flowers decorated her hair and body. She was all kinds of cute and tiny. So small she could fit in the palm of Peppa's hand.

"Are… are you a real fairy?" whispered Peppa.

"Are you a real giant?" squeaked the little fairy suspiciously.

Suddenly, Mrs. Bowers bellowed "Peppa!" from the other room, interrupting their awkwardly inquisitive introductions. "Where are you, child?" she boomed.

"Be right there, Mrs. Bowers!" she yelled back in a panic. She was in the wrong room talking to… a fairy!

"Can I take you with me?"

"No!" Saroja cried. "Are you going to eat me?!" shrieked the frightened fairy.

"Yuck! I'm not going to eat you, especially if you taste like that purple goop! But I don't think it's a good idea for you to be inside Mrs. Bowers' private room. She might think you're a bug and squish you with her duster or something. I can keep you safe right here in my pocket. No one has to know!" pleaded Peppa to the skeptical fairy.

"Peppa! If you don't come now, I will speak to your mama!" threatened Mrs. Bowers from the other room.

"We have to leave now!" warned Peppa.

With a quick, frightened nod, the fairy flew into Peppa's pocket, and they hurried out the door. The ten-year-old detective had found something most special. A fairy! But in her haste, she forgot her favorite thing… it lay on the floor by the window, pages rippled open for anyone to read.

The Safest Place I Know

"What happened to you, child?" blurted Miss Bowers when Peppa returned to the store's main room, all covered in dust. "You were supposed to throw out the trash, not roll around in it. Go on and use the washroom to clean yourself up, and get your little legs home. I'm gonna speak to your mama!"

That was fine by Peppa. She was eager to leave the market and meet her newfound friend. Besides, Mama was still at work, so the punishment would wait.

When she arrived home, Peppa scampered upstairs faster than a hound chasing a fox on a hot summer's day. She slammed the door behind her and quickly pulled the curtains shut.

"There!" she declared. "It's all clear for you to come out now."

Peeking out from her pocket, the little winged fairy stretched and gave a good look around the room before fluttering about. Searching for a place to rest, she settled upon a pink bow atop Peppa's dresser and gave a whizzing sigh of relief.

"OOH WEE, that was close!" agreed Peppa. "I don't know what I'd have said if Mrs. Bowers had seen you! She's known for sussing out situations when it doesn't seem right. A real life fairy?" Peppa was beside herself with excitement. She spoke so fast her tongue could barely keep up with her lips.

"I'm Peppa and this is my house and my room. My grandparents are downstairs so we have to be extra quiet. Are you hungry? I have tootsie rolls in this candy stash right here in my tent."

Offering a bit of the chocolate to the fairy, Saroja took one sniff and sat back down. "You eat this instead of berries?" asked the fairy with her nose scrunched up.

"Instead of fairies," teased Peppa. The fairy took a step back. "Sorry, just a joke. I don't eat fairies, remember? Do you have a name?"

"I sure do, my name is Saroja."

"Saroja Fairy or Fairy Saroja? Which is better?"

The fairy finally broke a smile, and then the sweetest laugh that sounded like music. "Should I call you Peppa Giant?" she jested before doing a formal introduction. With a little bow, she declared, "I am Saroja from the enchanted land of Lumella."

Now it was Peppa's turn to laugh. "I'm not a giant. Just a human, and not even a big one," she winked. "Sa-ro-ja. That was the name on the book. Do you live in that book?" queried Peppa.

"No," the fairy giggled. "Saroja means Lotus. I'm named after it. I live in a place far from human view, where rivers and rocks sparkle with crystals and gems, shining a light so bright it would fill any child up with wonder."

"Where is this place?" blurted Peppa, suddenly needing to see this land more than anything she had ever needed in her busy ten years of living.

"Humans aren't allowed," said Saroja plainly.

"Not even friends?" chirped Peppa.

"Friend? What is a friend?" asked Saroja.

"A friend is someone who you tell your best jokes to, someone who says nice things and is honest when things aren't right. Grandma Nelly says a good friend is hard to find, and you have got to be the hardest."

"Friend… we have friends in Lumella. We call them Lyntalla."

"Then you are my Lyntalla," smiled Peppa, proudly offering her hand to shake.

"You are my friend," replied Saroja, grabbing onto Peppa's pinky. Now, trust is a funny thing between first time friends. It binds you in spirit and love. At that moment, Saroja decided to trust Peppa entirely.

The Lotus Flower

"Lumella is secretly nestled in the woods among the tall oak trees surrounded by a beautiful bed of poppies," Saroja told her eager audience of one. "But someone removed the invisible veil and stole our sacred Lotus flower."

"Why would someone want to steal it?" Peppa was whispering again. It sounded like top-secret stuff.

"The Lotus flower is special because it keeps the balance of light and dark as it binds our world to yours, Peppa. Just as the sun sets and rises each day, so does the Lotus. It has a magical pink aura that hides us from prying eyes, and helps us to heal the land from human waste and destruction."

"Can it heal people?" sparked Peppa with a thought.

"Yes. It can heal anything, with permission from the Fairy Goddess, of course," clarified Saroja.

"Fairy Goddess…" Peppa echoed, but her mind traveled downstairs to her sick grandfather lying in his bed. Had she found a cure? Would it be too much to ask to borrow the flower?

Saroja continued, "I came here to find the Lotus and bring it back to my home. I'm afraid I can't do it though. This world scares me, Peppa. I hid inside that mean man's basket to escape the night's storm."

"A mean man?" buzzed Peppa.

"Yes, the one who left the basket out in front of the market. He went inside to speak with the lady of the shop. When she opened the door at daylight, I flew inside."

Saroja explained to Peppa that her family had been charged with guarding the Lotus, and they had all gone missing looking for it. The Enchanted Fairy Goddess had sent Saroja as a last effort to find it, and hopefully her kin. "You see, Peppa, I'm the last of my kind, a Faelyn that can bring the Lotus back and save our world," sighed Saroja.

"Not the only one. I could help you find it!" offered Peppa. "I'm really great at finding things. Grandma lost her reading glasses, and I found them under the seat of her car. Mrs. Bowers lost the keys to the pantry, and I found them in her apron pocket. And this morning I found a basket full of fruit that led me to finding you inside that book! We have to look out for one another, ya know, cause that's what Lyntallas do!"

"Thank you, my friend," fluttered Saroja at first. "But are you sure? It could be dangerous," she warned.

"Where do we start?" asked Peppa.

"Where all good stories start... in the book. That's the guide to caring for the Lotus."

"If it's a book for fairies, why's it so big?" Peppa asked skeptically.

"Well… there's a lot in it." Saroja responded, a bit defensively. "Anyway, that's why I went to the market. Whoever took the book probably took the flower. It's sure to be close by." Saroja stopped when she saw the look on Peppa's face.

Of all the things for Peppa to forget - a book - her favorite thing in the whole world! She was so distracted by meeting Saroja, she left the fairy's big red book back at Mrs. Bowers' reading room.

"Well, Saroja, I guess we're going back to the market," groaned Peppa.

The Quest

So, the two Lyntallas made an everlasting pact. Saroja promised Peppa that if she could help her find the magical Lotus, she would make an exception and take her to meet the Enchanted Fairy Goddess in the land of Lumella. Peppa happily agreed, wondering at the chance to see the little fairy's world.

Saroja was desperate to get back to her quest, so Peppa hurriedly got dressed in her favorite pair of comfy overalls and running sneakers. She motioned for Saroja to once more hide in her pocket. Peppa then crept down the stairs and darted out the front door, kicking up dust once more along Old Dale Road.

Peppa began to run along the worn path with Saroja now flying beside her. She ran and ran as fast as she could to keep up with her new fairy friend. They needed to get into the market and the magical reading room without being seen. They arrived at the front of the store to spot

Mrs. Bowers' car parked outside the botanical shop next door.

"Let's go around the back," directed Peppa.

They shuffled behind bins and mailboxes, being careful not to be seen until they got to the window of the reading room that faced a quiet shadow-filled alleyway. The sun was still alive and vibrant, but so was the wind. Through a small crack in the window it puffed apart the velvet curtains allowing the two detectives a peak into the room as the wind chimes sang. Saroja flew in quickly but stopped just as sudden.

"It's gone!" she fretted.

Just then another gust of wind, heavier than the last, smacked Saroja in the face near knocking her off the ledge she was perched on.

"Next door," she squawked. "I… I can smell it. Hurry!"

Peppa didn't wait to ask. Saroja had caught a scent and wasn't about to lose it. They entered the adjacent alleyway which was filled with garbage. It was littered with moldy food, broken pots… and worse. Flowers and plants were thrown about, starving for water and care - a horrific sight for Saroja.

"Who would do such a thing?" she asked.

"Him," said Peppa.

Inside a well-kept shop, neatly filled with rare plants and herbs and colorful flowers, they spied Mr. Lawless. He was a tall man in multi-pocketed trousers, green smudged vest, and a floppy hat. A white scruffy beard hid a sly smile. Mr. Lawless was talking to Mrs. Bowers and…

"That's the bad man with the basket. He has the book!" squeaked Saroja.

Hiding behind Mr. Lawless' back was the Book of Saroja from Mrs. Bowers' reading room. Did she know, wondered Peppa? Or had he stolen it? It seemed there was more to Mrs. Bowers than Peppa first believed, but that mystery would have to be solved another day.

Suddenly, the little fairy became so afraid she began to shake in Peppa's hand, so much so that Peppa began to worry about what she had gotten herself into. She wanted adventure, but she also wanted to be able to go home when the adventure was over.

"Why are you so scared, Saroja?" whispered Peppa. "You have magic. You can defeat anything, right? Besides, I'm here with you, and we can get that Lotus back together. We're Lyntallas."

Saroja felt comforted by Peppa's words and her company. "Lyntallas," she repeated. Before she could say

anything else in response, the young human cried out.

"Look!" Peppa pointed towards a brand new sign hanging in the window. It read: **Auction Today, Rare Find Inside.** It had a familiar painted image, one that was on the book. "If that giant sign with a picture of a Lotus isn't a clue, then I don't know what is," Peppa sassed.

"Yes!" exclaimed the fairy. "That's it!" She began to fly inside.

"Wait! You'll get caught if you go in now," warned Peppa.

And so they waited, looking for their chance. Soon after Mrs. Bowers left, the two watched Mr. Lawless quietly as he tended to the flowers in his shop, preparing them all for one grand sale. Peppa knew Mr. Lawless was up to something, and none of it good. Up high on the top shelf, she noticed several peculiar glass jars with little locks on them. Small, sparkling creatures seemed to buzz about inside them.

"Are those dragonflies?" Peppa asked at first. "No... Saroja, look! In those jars!"

"Faelyn," cried Saroja. "He has my family!"

Sure enough, within each glass prison was a different fairy, adorned in wilted berries, leaves, and moss. But that wasn't all. There was one who was not held prisoner. They spied a tall, majestic fairy flying around the shop, tending to the most exotic plants. White paint on his body marked him as royalty.

"That's Jubi!" gasped Saroja. "He's one of the elders and the brother of the Fairy Goddess. Jubi went missing long before the Lotus disappeared!" Could Jubi have betrayed them? It was unthinkable to Saroja, but then Mr. Lawless moved a potted lily, and there it was. The Lotus. Jubi fluttered nearby.

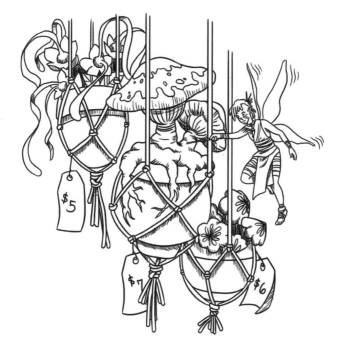

This must be what happened to her family. It all made sense now. No human had come into their world and stolen it. Jubi had taken it, and when her family had found the Lotus, Jubi had helped capture them.

Saroja knew that his magic was most powerful and fighting him would be very dangerous, but what other choice did she have? She felt in her heart that it was her destiny to free the other fairies and bring her namesake Lotus back to its rightful place. She had to be brave.

"I have a plan," she said. "Get ready to do a lot of talking."

"That, my friend, I can do," grinned Peppa.

Be Stronger Than Your Fears

It sat alone in a simple pot in the center of the room, where each ray of afternoon light could find it. It looked like the sun, with petals soft and pale, stretching back to its reflection in the sky. With a warm pink glow, the Lotus flower radiated. And waited.

"Hey, Mr. Lawless. It's a beautiful morning, isn't it?" beamed Peppa, interrupting Mr. Lawless as he was gazing at his prize.

She stood at his door, her best smile on full display. It was the smile that would make her brothers run. The smile that meant trouble. Something was afoot.

Startled by his unexpected guest, he replied with a huff, "Yes, it is, but the store is not open to the public today. We are having a private auction. You have to leave."

Ignoring his request, Peppa continued, "My, my, my… THAT is a mighty pretty flower you have over there, Mr. Lawless!" She clumsily pointed to the Lotus, knocking over a broom that caused a big commotion. Peppa spun around and around like a tornado into the store pointing to this flower and that, with Mr. Lawless trying desperately to catch whatever Peppa knocked over.

This made time for Saroja to appear with her pouch of pixie dust and throw it on Mr. Lawless. He fell asleep instantly and collapsed on the floor.

"Impressive," a voice goaded from behind the Lotus flower. "But it won't be enough."

"Jubi! Why are you doing this? Keeping the Lotus here will destroy Lumella. It will destroy our home!" Saroja screamed.

"It's the only way to save our home! This is no place for a young Faelyn to be," scoffed Jubi. "The Fairy Goddess shouldn't have been so weak as to send a child instead of coming herself!" Suddenly, Jubi hurled a pouch of withering dust.

Peppa swatted the dust away with Mr. Lawless' broom, saving Saroja just in time.

"I see you have a human pet, too," he mocked.

"I am Lyntalla," yelled Peppa as she tried to whack him, but he was just too fast.

"Humans can't be friends," sneered Jubi. "They ruin everything they touch. This old fool thought he was going to sell the Lotus flower to make an elixir."

Jubi chased Saroja and Peppa chased Jubi, whizzing around the store, in and under, through and over, planters and dangling chains, twine hampers, and wobbly tables. Faster and faster they moved until Peppa couldn't see them any longer except for the dazzling dust they hurled at each other, which crackled and fizzled. Jubi, who had a

better knowledge of Mr. Lawless' shop, forced Saroja to the hottest part of the store. At the last moment, Jubi darted left as Saroja banked right, and she flew straight into a cactus! Luckily, she missed all the prickly bits, but now he had her trapped.

Jubi pulled his wand, which was forbidden to use in battles against other fairies. "Go in the jar, Saroja, like your Faelyn kin. Or I will hurt your human Lyntalla."

"Why are you helping this man?" begged Saroja.

"I would never help a human, not anymore. I used him to try to lure out my sister. Humans do not care for this world, Saroja, this Earth, so why should we? I will take our flower and Lumella far away, where we can live and grow as we are meant to," he confessed.

"But… they need us," cried Saroja.

"They do not deserve us," stated Jubi.

"No!" Saroja took her own wand out.

"You wouldn't dare," he taunted.

But she did. She poured all of her essence into her wand and let go her only shot.

"Bullseye!" yelled Peppa, as a single ray of pink magic hit Jubi square in the chest. Jubi's wings fell like ashes to the ground, and then, so did he.

"You will pay for what you've done," he promised. The fairy prince then quickly gathered his crumbling wings into the shadows and slipped through a crack in the floor.

"Good riddance!" cried Peppa as she quickly grabbed the Lotus. Saroja knocked over the jars holding her family, setting them all free.

"We did it! You can go home now, Saroja! You can all

go home now!" exclaimed Peppa.

"We can, Peppa. We can all go to Lumella," Saroja beamed.

Saroja's family surrounded her, marveling at how she could have defeated Jubi. But there was one very important thing that Jubi had not taken into account while helping Mr. Lawless. The longer he stayed in the human world, the weaker his magic became, for just like the Lotus, and all of the elements of nature, its environment had to be just right to survive.

When old Mr. Lawless woke up, he didn't know what had hit him. His magical Lotus was gone, and so were the fairies, not that he would have remembered. Fairy dust, you see, will make you forget what you have seen or heard, and Mr. Lawless was covered in it.

Past the Cotton Fields and into the Woods

Saroja and the Faelyn collected herbs from different plants in the forest, rosemary, lavender, primrose, red berries and sunflower roots. They began to make an ancient mixture that would allow Peppa to enter Lumella, and more than that...

Saroja uttered some old words Peppa did not know, and offered her human friend a bowl of folded leaves in which a rainbow liquid sparkled. "You have to drink this if you want to see and hear our world," said Saroja, "and feel it," she added.

With much hesitation, Peppa gave it a good sniff and squished up her face in disgust. "Yuck! This doesn't smell sweet enough to taste!" she cringed. "It's worse than the purple goop!"

"You are funny, Peppa," laughed Saroja. "You have to drink it down before the sun sets. It's the only way inside."

Peppa cupped the floral bowl in her hands. She shut her eyes tight, and in one big gulp swallowed the whole thing down. When she opened them, her world had changed. "I don't feel any different. Hey, how come you've all grown taller than me? And why are the trees so big… and what's that buzzing sound… and how is everything speaking all at once?"

"It will take some getting used to, Peppa, but you are a part of Lumella now," smiled Saroja.

Peppa was nearly at a loss for words. Nearly. "Which part?" she asked. "The good part I hope. So I'm smaller. Did I get wings?"

"Erm… Excuse me, excuse me," interrupted a panicked voice in the distant brush. "Excuse me!"

"Who said that?" asked Peppa, already running in the direction of a giant oak tree within a bed of bright red poppies. She jumped over twigs and dodged swaying flower stems, trying to avoid bees as big as her as they flitted about, collecting pollen.

"Down here," replied a quivering voice. "I'm stuck!"

There, past the brush, was One Black Hare with his foot stuck within the roots of the old grand oak.

"How'd you get stuck like that?" asked Peppa.

"This old tree's got a hold of me and won't let go!" shrieked the hare.

"Don't be silly," said Peppa. "Trees can't hold you, and how are you… talking?"

"Well… it's not that simple," objected the old oak tree. "He was stealing from me."

"I was not," ruffled the hare. "I was hopping along, minding my way, when your root stuck its… root out and tripped me over. I fell, *without grace* might I add, mouth wide open, and landed right on top of all these acorns."

Peppa couldn't believe what she was seeing AND hearing. It was one thing to find a fairy and her entire family, another to hear voices speaking to her from both a hare and a tree! Plus the hare's fibs were worse than her youngest brother's (which always included a dog they didn't even have).

Saroja flew up to the great trunk of the wise oak and asked what the black hare needed to do to be released. The tree's face was full of knotted bark that resembled one of Grandpa's kind old friends, Peppa thought.

"What I need is a confession of truth from the hare," boomed the tree. "And an apology would be nice. It took me hundreds of years to grow those acorns."

"Alright, alright," whimpered the hare. "I haven't eaten for days, and neither have my little kits. I'm sorry, great tree. Please forgive me."

The tree not only unwrapped his arm-like branch

from the hare, it lifted another, revealing a second stash of acorns. "For the little kits," he rumbled, softer now. "When you need help, just ask, and if I can, I will."

"Thank you, I am truly grateful for your kindness, oh, wise and wonderful oak," proclaimed the hare, gathering up a few of the acorns. And then off he scampered into the woods with haste.

"Remember, dear ones, a thief will crumble at the sight of their own reflection. Or they will become better for seeing the error of their ways," imparted the wise oak.

And with that, a rainbow of light suddenly burst from the petals on the tree. It surrounded Peppa, the Faelyn, and all of the plants and flowers. The light grew brighter and brighter, revealing an opening within the belly of the old oak tree. It was a door of many colors, and a gateway to another world within our own. Saroja took Peppa by the hand.

"Are you ready?" she asked.

For the first time in Peppa's life, she could not speak. She was full, with joy and with wonder. All she could do was simply nod and smile and squeeze Sarjoa's hand tight.

Together with the healing fairies, Peppa stepped through the portal and entered into the mystical realm of Lumella.

Lumella

Saroja told Peppa that having a human child visit Lumella was a rare and special treat. The Faelyn went on to say it was the greatest reward for freeing them from the wicked Mr. Lawless and Prince Jubi. Surely, the Fairy Goddess would be happy to grant any wish of one so courageous as Peppa, she hoped.

Now, Peppa had done a lot of reading of fables and fairytales, but it was another thing seeing it with her own two eyes and on her own adventure. Lumella was even more beautiful than Peppa imagined. The rocks shined with glittering crystals. The trees and flowers were rich with color. And the scent… was fresh and clear. It was home to hundreds of fairies that lived in round houses made of sticks with rooftops of woven vines. They fluttered about their day, tending to flowers, plants, and their families. Lyntallas braided each other's hair. Proudly decorated with flowers and leaves, they used seeds to adorn sun-kissed skin, ever so unique and colorful by design.

It was both foreign and familiar at the same time for Peppa. Family is family no matter the place. Every fairy worked together in a harmonious rhythm, doing their best to take care of their beloved.

Much like children at play, they erupted in cheer at the sight of Saroja and the return of the lost Faelyn. As Peppa walked through a gathering crowd, each fairy caught her eye with a smile and a nod. They were so humbled and happy that Saroja and the human child had successfully completed the mission, saving the Lotus and their world. Overcome with merriment, a celebration of music and dancing was the only natural answer.

"Have a seat here," gestured Saroja to a rock under the leaf of a rose. "I want you to meet someone very special."

Peppa nervously sat as instructed, her eyes filling the frame of her glasses, trying to take in all that was happening before her.

The wind began to whistle a musical tune, and everyone turned toward a fluff of cotton floating in the air. It drew closer, revealing instead an elaborate white mane of hair atop a silk petal dress threaded in gold. The Enchanted Fairy Goddess had come. Peppa sat very still.

The Fairy Goddess hovered before the two heroes, her eyes smiled, twinkling in appreciation and affection. She presented them with a gracious bow of gratitude.

"Peppa, this is our Fairy Goddess," shared Saroja. "The Queen of Lumella. Azora."

"Sweet Peppa," said the Fairy Goddess, "I want to

thank you with my whole heart, as do all of us here in this land. You helped return our sacred Lotus and our beloved Faelyn."

"You're welcome," squeaked Peppa, immediately wishing she had said something more profound. The Fairy Goddess laughed with a kindness true and pure.

"Take this gift, my heroic girl." The Fairy Goddess then gifted Peppa with a silver necklace hung with a talisman. It was made from black volcanic glass. Heart-shaped, it mirrored the loving sentiment of this magical place.

"And to you, my sweet Saroja," she continued. "You have given us great honor, and I am filled with gratitude and love for your bravery. I will reward you with this crystal wand. It is specially crafted with amethyst and quartz."

The Fairy Goddess stretched out her arm, motioning for Saroja to place the Lotus back into its resting place. With the Queen's permission, she flew to the middle of the enchanted lake, lowering the delicate flower. It began to shimmer and then the most magnificent glow rippled across the water and the land. A burst of cheer rang throughout the world of Lumella.

"I think we're going to enjoy your company," smiled the Queen. "You are welcome to stay as long as you like."

"Miss Fairy Goddess…" fumbled Peppa, "I'd love to stay, but I have a very important question to ask you. My grandfather is very ill, and I couldn't bear it if I lost him. Can I use the healing powers of the Lotus to make him all better again?"

But before the Fairy Goddess could answer Peppa's

request, Jubi appeared from behind some tall blades of grass. He was defiant in his voice, but his body was still weak from battle and the loss of his wings.

"This is against our law, sister," he hissed. "I see since I've been away, you have taken to human children, even allowing them to sit within our sacred land."

"Our sacred land? Oh, my dear brother. Do not pretend to care for our home now. I know of what you've done," admonished Azora.

"What I've done is try to bring Lumella back to its rightful place, far away from this plane of Earth, far away from the ungrateful humans who do nothing but destroy their own world! We use our magic to mend it, but even the Lotus is not strong enough."

More than a few cheers rang out in defense of Jubi. There had been a quiet rebellion amongst a few of the Faelyn to flee the Earth plane. Peppa was dismayed about the idea of the fairies leaving Earth, but even she knew folks didn't take care of the plants and lakes and seas like they should. Even though Jubi acted wrong, the words he spoke were right. As if echoing her fears, Jubi continued with a small part of a larger legend…

"Our lineage is intertwined throughout time and space. So, when the fairies of Lumella were summoned to the Earth many centuries ago, our mission was to help heal the people and the land. We had an agreement to teach the humans to harvest and grow plants, to look after the animals and little children. But along the way, promises were broken and our families were torn apart. Humans grew further away from nature and stopped believing in us fairy folk."

"But you captured my family!" cried Saroja, suddenly in anguish. "Maybe the humans have lost their way, but we have to help them find it, not abandon them!"

The Faelyn gasped! As much as the Fairy Goddess wanted to punish her brother for his clear betrayal of their land, she knew he was right, but so was Saroja. Looking down at Peppa, she saw an answer to the conflict.

"Peppa, what my brother is saying is true, but I cannot let your bravery go unrewarded. I will give you a choice. You can stay and be one of us... a true Faelyn. You can help us nurture the Earth. Or Saroja may take you and the Lotus back to your home to cure your grandfather, but if you do, there you will remain, and our world will be cut off. We will be forgotten to you, Peppa. Forevermore."

This was the most difficult choice Peppa had ever faced. Leaving her family to live in Lumella with the Faelyn sounded like fun. She would be a true fairy, a hero of her own fable yet to be written! But she would miss her family terribly, and even though she couldn't stand being around her brothers, she still loved them more than life. Above all, her grandfather needed her. And heroes, as Peppa knew, made sacrifices to do the right thing.

"Thank you, Fairy Goddess. It's a tough choice and I really want to stay, but… I need my grandpa to be better again," said Peppa. Some of the Faelyn cheered Peppa's decision, while Saroja sorrowfully accepted it. Behind them all, Jubi skulked away, and some of the Faelyn followed.

"Very well, child. The Faelyn of Saroja will escort you both, but please heed this caution, as the flower is still weak. Promise me you will use its healing magic once, and once only. Otherwise, you risk destroying it and our world, and everything we are will die with it."

"I promise," Peppa nodded.

Saroja and Peppa's adventurous quest seemed to come to an end as quickly as it had started. No human child had ever been to the land of Lumella and returned to tell about it. Well… one had, but that is a tale for another time.

The Journey Home

It was dusk when Saroja and Peppa set off on their journey back to the world of humans. Violet and white corkscrew clouds twisted like puffy marshmallows high above the two friends, pointing the way home. Saroja's own family accompanied Peppa as her honor guard. Unlike the journey to Lumella, the return was rather quiet. No one wanted to admit this was going to be the final farewell.

It was all too quiet. And silence made Peppa uncomfortable. She was only a mile away from Old Dale Road, still small amid the tall grass, passing bugs and beetles for the last time. She would try and remember this moment forever once she returned to boring normal size, despite their "forget-me" magic. "Everything is so different now, I don't wanna forget!" she suddenly blurted.

"Maybe there is another way," offered Saroja. "Surely, we can figure something out."

"This is the only way, sister," stated Kadara, Saroja's

older brother. "It is the law of Lumella."

"You better listen to your elders," echoed a familiar sneer, followed by a disruptive buzzing sound. Jubi had followed behind with a tribe of his own, each wingless and riding on wasps. Jubi stared them down from atop the biggest one with a look of madness in his eyes. "It is time for the human and all her kind to forget. Do not risk the fate of our Faelyn for this one. The flower is too fragile. Give it to me and I will ensure its return to Lumella, for the safety of the Faelyn."

"Peppa made a deal to cure her grandfather first!" Saroja shouted.

"Not with me, she didn't," Jubi replied, pulling his wand. "Give me the flower or face my wrath!"

Saroja quickly drew her new wand to protect Peppa. "If you want it, come and get it!"

BANG! And so it began, as streaks of light suddenly whizzed and whirred with bangs and clangs as Jubi's tribe and Saroja's family zapped wands and hurled dazzling dust at each other.

"Take the flower home, Peppa. Hurry!" Saroja yelled as she blinded a wasp and rider with a well-aimed blast from her wand.

Peppa was already thinking the same thing, and scurried home as fast as her fairy-sized legs would carry her. If only she had wings! High above, the fairy battle carried on as they zoomed around trees and porch lights, flying up to the rooftops and back down again. Any human passing by would believe it was a furious dance of fireflies twinkling in the night.

"Hand over the Lotus. I am the rightful leader of

Lumella!" Jubi proclaimed with defiance. "I will restore it back to the land that it was before Azora took reign and ruined everything!"

"You are not the rightful leader of anything. You're just a thief!" cried Saroja, avoiding another bolt of magic.

"A thief," thought Peppa as she reached her front door. "A thief will crumble at the sight of his own reflection." She recalled the wise words of the old oak tree. Peppa had another decision to make, and a quick one at that. She could run and take the Lotus to her grandpa, or she could help her new friends who were risking their lives for her.

"Hey, Jubi! Look what I have, THE LOTUS!" Catching his attention, Jubi abandoned his fight with Saroja's tribe and flew at Peppa with lightning speed. Peppa gulped.

The fairy prince raised his wand back and unleashed all of his anger into one big magical blast. Grabbing the mirrored talisman from her necklace, Peppa held it directly out in front of her. Jubi needed to see the monster he had become. And he did. With the quickest flash of light, Jubi's eyes caught sight of himself. His soul was bare and almost rotten, as he had lost his beautiful vibrant glow. His flower adornments had withered, and his wings would never return. He screamed out an alarming wail, "What have I become?"

Before anyone could answer, the zap he had aimed at Peppa also bounced back off the talisman. It hit him in the chest and knocked him clean off the big wasp. Jubi fell to the ground and curled up like a child, pained by the fall

and his own reflection. The fighting stopped. He began to weep. He was dying of a broken spirit. He looked at Peppa with the saddest eyes she had ever seen and said only, "I am sorry."

The Healing Fairies

"This isn't right," pleaded Saroja. "We are family. Fighting each other goes against the very nature of our existence. We are healers of this land." She looked at Peppa with tears welling up. Peppa looked at the fairy prince as his life slowly slipped away.

Peppa wished silently that the Lotus had the power to save both Jubi and her grandpa. She was so close to home, to the man who had helped raise her, she could still run in the house and up the stairs and then… and then… But, if she healed Jubi… Peppa didn't want to wonder what would happen to her grandpa. She had made a promise to the Fairy Goddess who had warned her that she could only use the flower once, the flower Jubi had lost his mind fighting to protect.

"We are healers," Peppa echoed in whisper.

She slowly made her way to Jubi and knelt down beside him. She gently handed over the flower.

"But your grandfather…" Saroja sniffled.

"You need him," Peppa whispered in return.

Saroja took a deep breath and then placed the Lotus above his heart.

Saroja and Peppa and all of the fairies linked in a circle that surrounded Jubi with a loving embrace. The flower pulsed in a beautiful pink light and began to restore him. He was their Faelyn and would be given another chance to do right by Lumella and the Fairy Goddess, to do right by Peppa.

A Giving Heart Overflows with Love

They left Jubi in the care of his followers as the healing magic took hold and made their way into Peppa's house. Now they hovered like tiny floating lights above Peppa's grandfather, who lay asleep in his bed. It was nighttime, and a time for farewells. Peppa sat by his shoulder, and whispered, "I'm sorry, Grandpa. I tried."

"I'm sorry also, Peppa," said Saroja's brother, Kadara. "I'm sorry we cannot save him."

"Maybe we can." Saroja dried her eyes and spoke up. "The Fairy Goddess didn't say it could only work once, just that any more would risk destroying it."

"Which would risk destroying our home," Kadara reminded. "Our mission is to protect the Lotus."

"And Peppa saved the Lotus. If there's even a chance, we have to try!"

"No," said Peppa bravely. "Thank you, my Lyntalla, but your brother is right. As much as I want to, the Lotus connects your world to mine, and even though I won't remember you after this, the world needs you. The world needs magic. I can't take that from you."

"Good," said a humbled voice from the doorway. "Hopefully you won't have to."

Jubi flew into Grandpa's bedroom like a prince. He was more than restored. He was beautiful and radiant. Peppa was in awe. He looked like his sister, the Fairy Goddess, like royalty. His wings had grown, and he beamed with a bright light that canceled the dark. His followers had also regained their wings and their senses.

"You've proven me wrong, Peppa. You made a choice many would not, and you've shown me something I have forgotten. Hope. Hope for the human world.

"I share the same blood as my sister," Jubi continued. "I share my spirit with the Earth. Together, we will save him."

"But I promised the Fairy Goddess to use the flower once," said Peppa. "What will happen to Lumella?"

"We are healers," smiled Jubi. Peppa thought the room shone even brighter.

"Jubi is the Queen's twin," offered Saroja. "It may work, but the flower could use up all of Jubi's magic!"

"Bring the Lotus here please, Peppa," said Jubi calmly as he hovered over her grandfather.

"Are you sure?" asked Peppa.

"For the sacrifice you made for me, I am certain," he said.

Peppa looked at Saroja for guidance, and the fairy smiled through swollen eyes, giving her all the answer she needed.

Peppa handed the flower to Jubi, who softly lowered the Lotus into place. The flower was dry, and its leaves were worn. It had used most of its power and had been away far too long from its resting place in Lumella. "We will focus the healing energy together," commanded Jubi.

"Lyntallas?" said Peppa.

"Friends," winked Jubi.

And together they did. Forming a circle around Peppa's grandpa, they ignited the light of the Lotus. It beamed a magnificent radiance, creating a pink bubble of love and protection over the entire house.

"Look, it's working!" exclaimed Peppa. "Thank you, Jubi. Thank you, everyone!"

"Thank you, Peppa," said Jubi. "Without you, I would have lost my way forever. Many of us would. I will not forget you. You have reminded me what true magic is," Jubi said as he bowed low. "Magic is life itself."

"So… I guess it's time for me to forget you," said Peppa as she slumped on the bed. With tears in her eyes, she looked up at the fairy prince.

"Is it?" asked Saroja.

Grandpa lay fast asleep. In fact the whole house was in a deep sleep, dreaming of little winged creatures and dancing lights. It was the kind of dream you want to hold onto. They would wake up the next day feeling healthy and bright, never knowing the magic that was bestowed upon them and their home.

An Ancient Gift

When they all returned to the enchanted land of Lumella, Jubi had a different message for the Faelyn and his sister, Queen Azora. He spoke of the loving sacrifice he had witnessed and how Lumella would be poorer for losing a girl like Peppa. There had to be another way for Peppa to return to Lumella and stay with her family, he lamented.

The Fairy Goddess loved her brother, and knew he would return if the light was shown, but still she was moved. With the Lotus and all of the Faelyn safely home, her own magic bristled with energy. First, she restored all of Jubi's power and his place within the fairy queendom. The Faelyn of Lumella rejoiced to see the royal family reunited. But there were still a couple of Lyntallas who seemed sad, so the Fairy Goddess turned her attention to her brother's wish.

"Jubi is right. It would be a great loss."

Two pairs of watery eyes looked up at her, for there

on a toadstool sat Saroja and Peppa, sulking mightily.

"There is an ancient tradition, Saroja…"

"Yes, my Queen," the little fairy said, wiping her cheeks.

"Have you read the whole book?" asked Azora. The mention of a book got Peppa's attention.

"Umm… there's a lot…" admitted Saroja.

"Yes, I know. It's a big book. When I was young and it was in my charge, I managed to make it all the way to the end. All the way to the part about how the Lotus can bestow a gift upon a human who has shown great sacrifice in the name of love. It is the oldest custom and greatest gift that can be given to one who believes."

"It can?" stuttered Peppa, ever so curious to read the mysteries within the book.

"I know that chapter," smiled Jubi, incredibly pleased.

"And so it shall be," declared Azora.

The Fairy Goddess raised her wand to the sky and a wisp of colorful wind suddenly twisted and curled, surrounding Peppa. Faster and faster, for a moment she was hidden within the twirling rainbow. And just as fast, it vanished with a puff of smoke leaving behind a very changed girl.

Fairytales and Family

Within the enchanted land of Lumella, a smart, brave, inquisitive, and sassy-mouthed little girl sprouted wings.

Saroja's mouth was wide with surprise. Tripping on her own tongue, she exclaimed. "You're one of us, Peppa!"

"I'm a fairy?" the girl squealed, small once again.

"Well, sort of. You're something different. You're a Faelyn godmother!"

"A fairy godmother? But I'm only ten!" blurted Peppa.

"Yes, and you'll grow into it just right," laughed the Fairy Goddess.

The Fairy Goddess had many things to teach Peppa about their history, and her hopes for a brighter future. But she started with her gift. There are some rules to being a fairy godmother, you know.

"Now, Peppa, you have the ability to visit your family

and Lumella without any boundaries between us. You can shift from fairy size to human from now until forever, but every new moon, you must return to us. And make sure they forget, each time you leave."

"You got it!" promised Peppa, her brand new wings flapping with excitement. Azora wasn't so sure she would remember the last part, but she smiled as Peppa fluttered about.

And so, just as a sweet melody can travel through time and touch the heart of the old and young alike, Peppa would return home with her little flute and a lullaby to bring some magic to the world and dreams of adventure to the children she was charged with watching over.

Because even if her little brothers didn't remember her tales when they woke, they too would believe.

THE END

Aiysha Sinclair is a Healing Arts Practitioner, Fairyologist, and Film and Stage Performer. Her love for fairies and music began at a very young age. Influenced heavily by her Guyanese/Trinidadian roots, she learned folk stories and songs that held messages that preserved African and Caribbean culture. As an author, she aims to spark the imagination of both children and adults with fantastical tales of friendship, compassion, and healing.

Joyceline Furniss is a freelance digital artist from Long Island, New York, specializing in illustration and character design. She was the winner of the Niobe: She is Life #4 variant cover contest, and Saroja's Quest is her first illustrated book. When she's not drawing, she enjoys watching horror movies, reading, traveling, and spending quality time with her husband and cat.

The Enchanted Fairy Goddess
will return in Aiysha Sinclair's
YA novel

The Cotton Fairy

The Cotton Fairy

When the night shines blue
and the stars shine too
wait for me, wait for me
I'll be the one all dressed in white
I'll be the one who has taken flight
I'll be the one in the soft moonlight
wait for me, wait for me
We'll meet in the shadow of
the cottonwood
We'll live in peace as children should
wait for me, wait for me